StoryLand

Treasures

*Delightful Stories That
Teach Character Building
Lessons For Children*

Rod and Staff Books

(Milestone Ministries)
800-761-0234 or 541-466-3231
www.RodandStaffBooks.com

StoryLand

Treasures

Delightful Stories That
Teach Character Building
Lessons For Children

Karen Joann Miller

Ridgeway Publishing
Medina, New York 14103

STORYLAND TREASURES

First Printing - 2008
Second Printing - 2008
Third Printing - 2009

*For additional copies
visit your local
bookstore or contact:*

Ridgeway Publishing
3129 Fruit Avenue
Medina, New York 14103
(585) 798-0050 Ph.

Printed By:
Ridgeway Publishing

Illustrated by:
Laura Yoder

Cover Design:
M. Gagarin Design Services

Printed in the United States of America

ISBN# 978-0-9792009-4-6

Dedication

To all the many children who love to read stories and learn from .hem. To them I dedicate this book.

Acknowledgments

I Owe Grateful Thanks

To my parents, for their help and encouragement during the writing of these stories.

To my four brothers, for their advice and for providing incidents for the basis of some of the stories.

To my uncle and aunt, Norman and Marlena, for their patience. Without them, this book might never have been written.

Introduction

Welcome to *StoryLand Treasures*, a new book filled with wholesome stories that teach clear lessons. Lessons that instill solid character and virtue in children.

To all parents, let me assure you that reading is an effective means to influence children to do and live right. It is a good way to nurture and to mold their minds in righteousness, ever pointing them to God. Truly, this is a high and worthy calling.

Many lessons are taught in this collection of stories. Lessons that teach obedience, carefulness, kindness, gratefulness and more.

The origin of this book started when I read a story Karen was writing. As I read, I saw good potential and encouraged her to begin writing a number of simple stories that children would love to read and would teach a lesson at the same time. So, the stories began showing up one after the other. I was pleased, with what I saw, and I am sure you will soon understand why.

Finally, dear reader, you are holding in your hand the fruit of much labor and inspiration. This is Karen's first book. The first, I hope, of many more to come. I trust you will enjoy reading *StoryLand Treasures* as much as I enjoyed putting it together for you.

So now, sit back, relax and enjoy!

- Norman and Marlena Miller
Ridgeway Publishing

Table of Contents

1.

Cupcake Friends

Bang. Judith brought the lunch box down on the counter with a hefty slam. "Oh, I don't like school at all and I don't want to go tomorrow," she declared.

"Well, hello, and what a face!" Mother appeared from the sewing room, holding a dress in her hand. "Just tell me all about it," she encouraged.

"Oh, Mother," Judith frowned. "Ellen and Katherine are such good friends, and that would be alright," she added hastily, "but they just ignore me and I do want friends." The last words ended

Judith pulls a pan of cupcakes out of the oven.

in a wail.

Mother studied her daughter for a few minutes. "Why don't you look up Proverbs 18:24 and do what it says," she advised. "It has worked for many years and should work again. And, Mother changed the subject, please, bake a batch of chocolate cupcakes for the school lunches."

Judith nodded and pulled out a mixing bowl. As she gathered the ingredients together, she thought of what Mother had said.

Proverbs 18:24. Hmmm. That is probably, *A man that hath friends must show himself friendly.* And just like that another fragment of a verse flashed into her mind. *Heap coals of fire.*

Hmmm.

An hour later as Judith pulled pans of delicious smelling cupcakes from the oven, a thought burst upon her. "Why, of course," she said aloud.

"Mother," she called. "Could I decorate two cupcakes and take them along to school?"

"Why, yes," answered Mother without any hesitation. "You surely may."

Judith grinned. Mother knew.

The next afternoon the lunch box landed on the counter much more softly than the day before.

"Oh, Mother," Judith bubbled. "It worked, it actually did! I gave them a cupcake and they were so happy and friendly! Oh, we are going to have so many good times this school term. And... well, I should go change my school dress."

With that, Judith bounded from the room and ran up the stairs. Mother smiled a pleased smile.

2.

Learning To Be Grateful

"Esther," Mother called. "Esther, it's time to get up."

Esther rolled over in bed and hugged the quilt tighter around her shoulders. Suddenly she sat up with a start. Why, today was her birthday! Finally she was ten. Ten sounded very grown up, not like just nine.

Esther scrambled out of bed and into her clothes. Carefully she made her bed and smoothed the quilt, then she pattered downstairs.

"Good morning, birthday girl," Father smiled at

her.

"At last you're finally ten and you won't be saying you can't wait for your birthday every fifteen minutes," teased Nelson.

Esther grinned good naturedly. She suspected ten-year-olds didn't get upset at an older brother's teasing.

After breakfast was over Esther opened the gift that Father and Mother had given her.

First she pulled out a paint set. Esther looked at it and thought of all the hours she would spend in creating pictures. "Thank-you," she smiled. Then she peeped back into the bag.

"What...?" she reached in and pulled out a large pack of paper. "Paper?"

"It's card-stock," Mother explained, "Extra thick paper that works well for the painting that you like to do."

"Oh, I see. Thanks so much for my birthday gif', you thought of everything I'd need," Esther tried to express her appreciation.

"You're welcome," Mother assured her. "And now I'll let you out of the breakfast dishes if you want to try out your gift for an hour or so. And then you'll have to help me clean. We're having Grandpa and Grandma for supper this evening."

"Are we really!" Esther cried, "That will be fun! And thanks for letting me out of the dishes, I think I'm going to make a sunset," she opened the lid of the paint set. "I've been thinking of that for awhile already."

Esther hummed a tune as she plied her brush. I wonder what Grandpa and Grandma will bring me, she thought. I hope it's a new alarm clock, my other one quit working. Maybe I should have told Grandma that, then she'd know...

"Esther," Mother called. "Your hour is up. I need your help with the cleaning. Why don't you start in the kitchen."

"Aww," Esther frowned, "I was almost done."

"No grumbling," said Mother sternly, and Esther knew what would happen if she kept on. Esther swept the kitchen, then she dusted furniture and washed windows. There was plenty of work to be done and the afternoon flew.

Mother put a casserole in the oven for supper and brought the birthday cake out of the freezer while Esther combed her hair. Father and Nelson arrived home from work just before Grandpa and Grandma drove in the lane.

"They're here!" Esther called from the window as Grandpa and Grandma came up the walks. She ran to open the door.

"Hello, come on in," Esther said politely, but her eyes were on the plastic bag that Grandma was holding.

"What did you bring me Grandma? Is it a new alarm clock? My old one doesn't work anymore."

A rather surprised look came over Grandma's face. "I'm sorry, Esther. I didn't know that you needed an alarm clock, but I'll try to remember. I brought you a paint set." She smiled and held out the bag.

"A paint set!" Esther yelped, "But Grandma, Father and Mother already gave me a paint set this morning."

Now Grandma looked really surprised, "Why, Esther! I'm so sorry! I had no idea."

"That's alright," Esther hastened. "Don't feel bad."

Grandpa chuckled, "Do you think it will take until your next birthday to use both of them?"

"I doubt it," Esther managed. She took the bag from Grandma. "Thanks a lot."

"That's perfectly fine," Mother's voice startled Esther. "I know Esther will enjoy using your gift. Now you can come on into the kitchen, supper's ready."

After Grandpas had left that evening, Mother sat down with Esther. "I doubt I'll need to tell you that I was disappointed by your reaction when Grandma presented your gift. Just how do you think that made them feel? And asking what they brought you when they were barely inside the door was very impolite."

Esther hung her head. How ashamed she felt! She knew what she must do. She would apologize to Grandma the next time she saw her. Hopefully, that would help her remember to be more thoughtful from now on.

Spring

I love this time of year, don't you?
  When flowers say that winter's thro',
When grass is greening 'neath our feet,
  The sun is shining, giving heat.
The sky is blue, the clouds are white,
  And night sheds velvety moonlight,
The stars give glowing light o'rehead
  And moonlight bathes my cozy bed.
When birds burst forth with loud applause
  And sing merrily, of course, because,
The trees bedecked with robes of green
  Lend cheerfulness upon the scene.
When creeks run bubbling free of snow
  And gentle breezes softly blow.
When flowers bloom upon the farm
  We welcome spring with all it's charm!

3.

Birthday Lesson

"Happy Birthday, Calvin!" Mother greeted him as he came sleepily down the stairs for breakfast.

Birthday? Why sure enough! It was his birthday. His sleepiness was suddenly forgotten. This was the day he had been looking forward to for a long time!

"Do we have something special planned for my birthday?" he asked. Yes, he knew it wouldn't be polite to ask, but he felt he just could not help it.

Mother smiled. "Yes, we have," she answered, "Since we are having only a half day of school today, with so many leaving for Joe and Rachel's wedding, we thought we could go to the City Zoo and then have a picnic supper at the park!"

"Really?" Calvin's eyes shone. This was going to be fun.

"But remember, don't get your hopes up too far. It looks like it could rain," Mother said as she glanced out at the not-so-bright sky.

Calvin nodded, but the fact was, Mother's words didn't register as they should have.

All that morning at school, as Calvin bent over his schoolwork, images of funny monkeys and roaring lions danced before his eyes. He sighed. School seemed to go so slow all of a sudden.

It was almost noon when Calvin happened to glance up from his book.

What? Rain? Surely, oh surely not. But it was. It was coming down in a steady all day drizzle.

Calvin's shoulders sagged. What a short time of anticipation, only to have his hopes fall flat.

Mother met him at the door when he came home from school. One look at his disappointed face told her all that she needed to know.

"Change your clothes, Calvin," she said brightly. "I'm going over to Grandpas to get a quilt pattern and you may go along."

Calvin nodded. Going to Grandpas was fun, but after thinking and planning about a zoo trip?

"And we hope to make our zoo trip tomorrow if it works out," Mother called up the stairs after

Calvin and Grandpa roast marshmallows.

him.

Half an hour later Calvin slammed the car door and followed Mother up the flower lined walks.

"Why, Hello!" Grandma's cheery greeting lifted Calvin's spirits. "You are just in time for a snack." Grandma waved her hand at the glowing logs in the fireplace, throwing their light over Grandpa who was kneeling on the floor roasting marshmallows.

Calvin's eyes lit up as he found his place beside Grandpa.

"You know," he said quietly staring into the flames. "I thought it was almost too much for me to think about having my plans spoiled so soon. But now..." Calvin stopped.

"God knows best, son." Grandpa laid a worn hand gently on Calvin's shoulder. "And now you have tomorrow to look forward to. Always face disappointments with a smile."

Calvin stuffed a creamy marshmallow into his mouth and nodded his head vigorously.

Grandpa was right.

4.

The Lost Watch

Dawn wiped her dishtowel over the last cup and placed it carefully on top of the teetery stack. There! At last the dishes were done.

She would have just enough time to sweep the floor and read some more of the new book, *Joanna's Journey*, that her good friend Sheila had given for her birthday. She flipped her towel over a convenient chair on her way for the broom.

Grabbing it, Dawn flicked it across the floor with short quick steps. Instead of moving the rugs and chairs, she merely went around them. She couldn't even see the difference and she hoped Mother wouldn't either.

The screen door snapped shut with a sharp bang and Daniel entered carrying the empty milk bottles. "Mother said you are to put the potatoes on to boil and make some meat loaf for supper."

It wasn't her younger brother's fault, but Dawn glared at him anyway. Now she probably wouldn't have any time left to finish her interesting book. Well, it couldn't be helped.

Dawn swept her broom past the blue rug under the rocking chair. Something round and hard lay beneath it but she only pushed it further in and promptly forgot about it.

Dawn put the potatoes on to boil and an hour later when the family came to the supper table, it was neatly set and supper was waiting.

After supper, Darlene washed the dishes since Dawn had taken her turn yesterday.

Dawn skipped upstairs and rummaged through her drawers, looking for her puppy puzzle. Suddenly, she thought of something. Where was the little heart-shaped watch Grandma had given to her? It had to be around here somewhere. When her search brought no watch, she decided to go ask Mother.

Mother came out of the bedroom with baby Leon in her arms. She seated herself in the rocking chair as Dawn asked Mother about her lost treasure.

"Uhmm, let me think a minute," Mother answered as she gently rocked the baby.

Crunch!

"What was that?" Mother stopped. "Look under the rug, Dawn."

Dawn lifted a corner and peered underneath. "Mother!" she gasped in dismay. "My watch! And it's totally ruined!" She picked up the shattered glass and just stared.

"Oh! I am so sorry, Dawn," Mother exclaimed. Then she paused and thought a bit. "Did you lift the rugs when you swept the kitchen this evening?"

Miserably, Dawn shook her head as two large tears trickled down her cheeks.

Dawn sadly picks up her broken watch.

"If you would have done the job as you knew I wanted you to, this probably would not have happened."

Dawn nodded soberly as she dropped the fragments of the watch into the wastebasket.

"I am sorry, Mother," she said. "I will try to do a better job from now on."

"I am sure you will," said Mother.

Grandma's Coming

"Grandma's coming," cried the children,
  As they saw her driving in
Quickly straightened up the kitchen,
  Now the fun begins.

"Come right in," their mother welcomed
  As she hurried down the walk,
Children trailed along behind her,
  What a noisy stream of talk.

Did she know there were eight puppies
  In the kennel by the door,
Mother cat had blessed them rarely
  Fifteen, sixteen, maybe more.

Had she seen the flowers blooming
  In profusion by the lane,
They're the ones that Sister planted...
  Grandma's strength began to wane.

"Children, children," cried their mother
  As she ushered them away
"You must not be swamping Grandma,
  With your noise and talk today."

Grandma smiled so very sweetly
  (Tho' that was a sigh she heaved)
For she dearly loved the children
  Yet she must have been relieved.

5.

Working Together

Myron knelt beside the rabbit cage he was building. Carefully he fitted the door in place, then he reached for his hammer. To his disgust he saw that Marlin had it and was vigorously pounding in nails on his own rabbit cage that he was making.

"Give me that hammer," Myron demanded.

Marlin clung tighter. "I'm almost done with this side," he begged.

"Doesn't matter," Myron said peevishly. "I need it right now, so you had better hand it over quick."

"Well I'm not planning to. There's another hammer somewhere around here. You can use that one."

"I don't know where it is, and I don't have the time to search for it either. What's the matter with you? You selfish?" Myron growled.

Their voices rose louder and louder as the argument continued. It didn't take long to reach Father who was working just outside the shop. He plainly heard trouble and opened the shop door just in time to see Myron give Marlin a well delivered slap.

"Myron!" Father's voice was stern. "You know better than to hit your brother. I don't want you to do that again."

Myron felt instantly ashamed. He hadn't really planned on hitting Marlin, but suddenly he had just done it.

Father settled the dispute by sending Myron to find the other hammer, and after a few more words of warning Father went back to his work.

Myron bent over his rabbit cage, his thoughts churning miserably. *Whatever ailed me*, he thought, *to do such a childish thing as strike my brother.* "I'm sorry, Marlin," he said finally. "I shouldn't have hit you."

"That's okay," Marlin seemed embarrassed, "I should have given you the hammer."

Peace once more reigned in the shop as both boys worked on their cages.

Fifteen minutes later Father opened the shop door. "I need to get a part for the tractor in town. I'll be going right past Uncle Edwins. Shall I pick up your rabbits for you?"

"Oh yes!" Marlin cried.

"Please do," Myron added.

"Thank you, Father," both boys chimed.

"Are you about done?" Myron asked, half an hour later.

Marlin looked up from his work, "Only two more nails."

"I'm finished," Myron picked up his newly constructed cage and set it on the shelf. He picked up a piece of plywood and leaned it against the wall.

"You know," he exclaimed suddenly, "Lets clean up this shop. It's a mess."

Marlin put his cage beside Myron's and gazed about the shop. "You got that right. It should be cleaned. But I don't really feel like it," he admitted.

"Aww, come on. We don't have anything else to do until Father comes back. We might as well."

"I guess," Marlin consented, catching some of Myron's enthusiasm.

Myron picked up their hammers and the nails that lay scattered about. Marlin hung up the tools that cluttered the shelves and rolled up the leftover wire netting from their rabbit cages. Myron was just finished sweeping the floor, when they heard Father's pickup driving in the lane. Myron quickly hung up the broom and both boys ran out of the shop.

Father stopped the pickup at the shop and the boys clambered over the tailgate.

Myron lifted the cover of the cardboard box and two tousled heads peered eagerly inside.

"Ooh!" Marlin said under his breath, "Aren't they something!"

And they were. Four snow white rabbits with pink eyes, huddled together, in the straw in the corner of the box. Carefully the boys set the box on the ground. Marlin ran to the shop to get the rabbit cages and gently the boys put their new pets into their home.

"Put the cages behind the shop," Father picked up the part he had bought for the tractor and opened the shop door. "Well! It looks like someone has been busy!"

Marlin and Myron looked at each other. They had been so taken up with the rabbits, that they had momentarily forgotten about their surprise for Father.

"We were done with the rabbit cages and we saw that the shop needed to be cleaned," Marlin explained.

"You did a good job," Father smiled his approval, "Looks nice."

"That sure was a lot more fun cleaning up the shop, even if it was work, than squabbling like we were this afternoon, "Myron observed as he and

Marlin set their cages with their precious cargo behind the shop.

"It was," Marlin admitted. "I'm glad we did. Especially when I saw how it pleased Father."

Myron nodded. "It certainly was well worth it."

6.

Trapped!

Squeak. The kitchen door opened and Father came in. "Boys, it's time to start with your chores. Please, throw down the silage first and then help as usual with the milking."

Ronald nodded and dropped the jelly coated butter knife in the sink. His brother Reuben pushed the bread back into the bag and followed Father out the door.

"Wish we wouldn't have to do the chores earlier tonight," Reuben told his brother.

"Um-hum," Ronald agreed. "But since Father is going away after supper for a meeting, we might as well do them now and have Father to help us, than

39

do them later and alone."

The boys had reached the silo by now and their train of thought continued. After they had worked for several minutes, Ronald said, "You know, I just thought of a great idea. If we would throw down enough silage to last us for several days, we wouldn't have to do this every evening."

"Say, a bright idea!" Reuben said admiringly. "Let's do it."

So the two boys got to work. On and on. Forkful after forkful of silage went down the chute.

"Whew, I am getting hot!" Reuben muttered. But as he thought of tomorrow's free time, he only worked faster.

"Okay," Ronald said finally. "Let's see if we have thrown down enough."

"Ronald." Reuben's voice dripped with disbelief. "I can't see any hole down there anymore. The silage has piled up too far!"

"What! Are you sure? I can't believe it. I am going to back down the ladder to make sure."

With that Ronald backed down as far as he could go. Sure enough, there was no exit. Ronald fairly flew back up to Reuben and said, "We had better call for help. We are trapped!"

With one voice that became more desperate with each yell, they called at the top of their lungs.

"Help, h e l l p, h e l l l p!"

Ronald began to beat on the metal sides of the chute, but that did no good.

Both boys kneel down to pray for help.

They were too far away. Nobody could hear them.

Then both boys began to cry.

Suddenly, Reuben's face lighted up. "I know what! Let's pray."

So both boys knelt down and Reuben prayed first, "Jesus, we are trapped here in the silo and we can't get out. Will You please help us out of here quickly before it gets dark? Amen."

Then Ronald prayed, "Lord Jesus, You can see that we are trapped in here and nobody can hear us. Will You please send help soon? In Jesus Name we pray, Amen."

No sooner had the boys looked up, when Ronald said, "You know I just thought of something. We can't walk around the top. That would be too dangerous. Why don't we try to dig ourselves out?"

"Hey, great idea!" said Reuben.

With that encouragement, Ronald went back down the ladder as far as he could go and began to dig. Silage flew as he dug deeper and deeper.

"Say, I think I see some light," Ronald whispered to himself. The sliver of light became a hole. A hole about as big as his head.

"I think I can make it if I kick my way through," he called to Reuben. With one final kick he slid out of the chute with Reuben right behind.

Once outside, they stood staring at the huge pile of silage they had thrown down while breathing deeply of the fresh air. What an experience!

"You know," Reuben broke the silence. "Don't you think we should have left some up there," he looked up at the tall silo looming above him. "For tomorrow afternoon?"

"Yes, I rather think we should have," Ronald admitted. "You don't think anybody saw what happened, do you?"

Later that evening, at the supper table, as the boys related their tale, they found that Father already knew what had happened.

"It seems that Grandpa saw you dig yourself out of your predicament and found it rather amusing," Father's eyes twinkled as he continued. "From now on be thankful you have a healthy body so that you can chore and appreciate work. Also, that could have been very dangerous if the silage had piled up so far you could not have dug your way out."

"God was very good to you to help you out of the silo. You did right by calling to God for help. He is faithful and wants to help His children at all times."

Both boys nodded their head soberly. They felt a deep thankfulness for having such an understanding and concerned father.

"Yes," Reuben said, "God was very good to us. And I know one thing, I have learned a good lesson. From now on I want to be more careful and use more foresight."

"Same here," echoed Ronald.

7.

Josiah Learns to be Kind

"Josiah," Mother called. "Come here a minute."

Josiah looked up from the birdhouse he was nailing together. "Yes? What do you want?"

"I am afraid I saw Diamond running across the lane a minute ago. See if you can put him back in. We don't want trouble with our neighbors if he goes over there." Mother went back to her work and shut the door.

"Oh, that bothersome horse," Josiah growled. "Just *how* could he get out again? I just fixed the fence." He put his bird house down and started running in the general direction of the neighbors. "I'll have to tie that pony to a pole if he persists in running away, at least I haven't seen a fence yet that could hold him. He always manages to find a hole or else he just makes one."

Josiah slowed down as he neared the neighbors. He did not see any vehicles and he knew that the young couple that lived there both had jobs away from home during the day, so he ran around the house.

"What!" he stopped short. Evidently the Wilsons had just bought a new horse, and what a horse! He wasn't handsome but he was big and he was not on friendly terms with Diamond in the least.

Josiah knew he had to do something quick to save his little pony or the fence might not hold much longer. He grabbed a stone and ran at the fighting steeds. It was becoming more evident that Diamond was on the losing end and it made him angry. "Hey!" he yelled, "What do you think you are doing?" He hurled the rock with all of his thirteen-year-old strength and hit the big horse smartly on the shoulder.

This was a new attack and the horse snorted and reared up on his hind legs. Josiah saw his chance and rushed in to grab Diamond by the halter. Diamond was reluctant to abandon the fight but Josiah tugged and pulled until Diamond followed.

"Just *what* do *you* think you are doing?" Mrs. Wilson's angry voice astonished Josiah. He did not have any idea that she was around, but there she was, as big as life, peering out the window.

"Why, I just came over to get my pony," Josiah stammered, he berated himself for being so shook up.

"You had no reason to throw that rock at my horse. Cruel! That's what I call it." Mrs. Wilson was huffing with indignation. "And if you knew what was good for you, you'd get off this property right this minute!" The window went down with a crash.

Josiah stood there stunned. Then as the full impact of her words sank in, he figured he ought to obey and started running out the lane pulling Diamond along behind him. He slowed down when he reached the road. "Whew! That woman had a lot of steam!" he muttered. "And that horse of their's, he looks awfully mean, almost chewed Diamond up. I'd guess he deserved that stone."

Josiah led Diamond back to his field and securely shut the gate. Then he walked to the house. He poured a glass of cold water and plunked into a chair.

"Did you bring Diamond back?" Mother wondered as she ironed another shirt.

"Yes."

"Did you have any trouble?" Mother asked instinctively.

"Perhaps I did." Then Josiah proceeded to tell her all about the scene.

"What am I to do now?" he wondered when he finished.

Mother sighed. "We don't want to ruin the good relationship we have had with our neighbors so far. Do you have any idea how to better the situation?"

"Go and apologize," Josiah said quietly.

"I am baking pies this afternoon," Mother said. "My advice would be to..."

"Take one of those pies as a peace offering," Josiah finished.

"Yes," Mother said. "And whatever you do, don't go throwing anymore stones at horses or any animal for that matter, and certainly not the neighbor's."

"I won't," Josiah promised. "I guess I got kinda mad."

That afternoon Josiah knocked sheepishly at the neighbor's door, a still warm apple pie in one hand.

Mrs. Wilson opened the door. She scowled when she saw Josiah.

"I am really sorry for losing my temper this forenoon and throwing that rock at your horse. It won't happen again. Here is an apple pie for you," Josiah said all in one breath.

Mrs. Wilson softened as she eyed the boy on her doorstep. "That is alright. Thanks for the pie," she said as she took it.

"Well that wasn't too awful," Josiah decided as he walked home. "Sometimes it seems I need to learn a lesson or two the hard way."

8.

Robert Learns His Manners

Mother let her dirty dishwater swirl down the drain as she hung up her dishtowel. "There that's done. Shall I help you get that side finished, Grandma?"

Mother pulled out a chair and sat down beside Grandma. Their needles softly moved through the brightly designed quilt as they talked.

Clatter, Clatter, Thump! Six-year-old Robert burst into the room. He shoved his way in between Grandma and Mother and held up his toy truck for inspection.

"Look!" he cried. "The back wheel came off!"

Mother frowned. "Robert, Grandma and I were talking. You must not interrupt like that."

"Oh." Robert looked ashamed. "I'm sorry, Grandma." He wiggled away from the quilt and stood at Mother's other side.

"Now," Mother said as she took the truck. "Where is the wheel?"

Robert gave it to her and she popped it back into place. He took it and ran to the toy box.

"Robert," Mother called. "What else?"

Robert stopped. "Thank you, Mother, for fixing this," he said sheepishly.

Mother nodded and smiled as she said warmly, "You are welcome, Robert."

Several days later the family was gathered around the supper table.

"I want some strawberry jam," Robert called impatiently. "I asked twice already."

"Robert, what should you say?" Father asked.

"Please, could I have some strawberry jam?" Robert repeated his question politely as he knew Father wanted him to.

"Sure," Father replied as he handed the jam to him.

"Manners are such a fuss." Robert sulked over his mashed potatoes and gravy.

"Robert," Mother chided. "Good manners are good habits and are a sign of respect."

Robert enjoys his delicious lollipop.

Robert nodded soberly. "I am sorry. I will try to do better."

Weeks passed, and one day Father needed to buy some nails at the hardware store. Robert was pleased to be allowed to go along and followed Father through the store looking at the brand new hammers and the sharp nails, with shining eyes.

"I think this is the size we need," Father remarked as he picked up a box of nails and strode to the counter to pay.

"Oh." Robert stopped. There beside the cash register was a plastic can filled with lollipops. Robert's mouth watered. He knew how good those were!

The clerk placed the nails in a paper bag, then she glanced down at Robert's wishful eyes.

"Would you like a lollipop, Sonny?" She offered him one and he took it eagerly.

Suddenly he remembered. "Thank you," he said bashfully.

"You are welcome," she smiled.

Father slammed the truck door shut and placed the nails on the floor.

"I was very glad you remembered your manners," Father said as he turned the key.

"I am, too," Robert agreed as he pulled off the wrapping and took his first delicious lick. "Please and Thank You don't seem such a bother after all."

Father nodded and smiled.

9.

Telephone Manners

The sewing machine whirred as Cynthia skillfully guided the material. The flashing needle left a neat row of stitches across the hem of her new dress skirt. Suddenly she paused and cocked her head. Sure enough the phone was ringing.

Cynthia got up from her chair. "Shall I answer it, Mother?"

"Yes, please," Mother wiped her floury hands on her apron, and turned back to her bread dough, meanwhile keeping one ear tuned to the conversation.

Cynthia lifted the receiver. "Hello?..no, this is Cynthia...no...what?...yes...bye." Cynthia hung up the phone and turned to Mother. "That was Aunt Denise, and she asked if you were available. When I said you weren't, she told me she'll call you back later."

"Oh, Cynthia," Mother looked a little shocked. "You mean when Aunt Denise asked if she could speak to me, you just said, 'no', and didn't give any explanation?"

Cynthia nodded.

"Cynthia, Cynthia," Mother chided. "You are thirteen and old enough to have better telephone manners."

"But Mother, I was in a hurry to get back to my sewing."

"I'm afraid that is not much of a valid excuse. Your sewing is not so important that you can't take time to be polite. From now on I'd like if you'd say your name when you answer the phone, like this, 'Hello, Masts, Cynthia speaking.' "

"Oh, Mother! Do you really mean it?" Cynthia cried in consternation," I don't think I could. It sounds too much like a secretary at the dentist office."

"I mean it," Mother said firmly. "And while we're on the subject, I also want you to offer to take a message if Father or I are not available right away. And please, always say 'good-by' properly, instead of just 'bye'."

Cynthia heaved a sigh and went back to her sewing.

Rr-rr-ring!

"Oh, no," Cynthia muttered under her breath, "Can you get it, Mother?"

"I'm sorry, Cynthia, but I'm changing the baby's diaper. You'll have to."

Rr-rr-ring.

Cynthia knew Mother expected her to put her crash course of telephone manners to good use. Nervously she picked up the phone, "Hello, Cynthia, speaking Masts," she said clearly. Immediately she felt engulfed in a warm wave of embarrassment. Had she really said that? Oh, surely not!

"Um, hello Cynthia, this is your neighbor, Mr. Reynolds. Is your father there?"

"He's not here right now, but can I take a message?" Cynthia looked sideways at Mother and could see that she was doing her best to hide her big grin.

"Yes, please, just have him call me back once he gets in. Thank you. Good bye."

"Good bye," Cynthia answered and hung up the phone.

"Oh, no!" Cynthia cried and dropped into the nearest chair. "I just can't do it, I knew I couldn't. Did you hear what I said?"

"Yes, I heard," Mother laughed cheerily.

"I didn't mean to. All the way to answer the phone I was repeating what I should say and then it came out like that. And Mr. Reynolds is such a very polite, refined business man. What must he think?"

"You just need more practice, that's all," Mother assured, once she could speak again.

"I don't want to ever try again," Cynthia mourned. "That was awful."

"Don't look at it that way," Mother said, "If at first you don't succeed, try, try again."

The next afternoon the phone rang once again while Cynthia was doing the dishes.

Mother smiled at Cynthia from where she was making pies and by that Cynthia knew that she would have to answer the phone.

Cynthia picked up the receiver a little apprehensively. "Hello, Masts, Cynthia speaking," she said properly.

"Hello, Cynthia. This is Aunt Denise. Is your mother available?"

"She is baking pies right now. Would it be alright if she would call you back in about ten minutes?"

"That would be fine, Cynthia," Aunt Denise said. "Thank you, good by."

"Bye, I mean, good by," Cynthia said hastily, and hung up the phone.

Mother looked up from her pies with a smile. "You're getting better and better at it," she encouraged.

After several weeks it became natural for Cynthia and how thankful she was for her mother who had taken the time to teach her polite telephone manners.

10.

Haste Makes Waste

"Melody," Mother called. "I'd like if you'd wash the dishes and sweep the kitchen floor yet before Father comes home."

Melody looked up from her book and groaned silently. It seemed to her that there was constantly so much work, and this book was begging to be read. Melody sighed grumpily and laid the book down on the couch. Reluctantly, she ran hot water in the sink and plunged the water glasses into the snow-white suds.

Melody glared out the window, it seemed there were dishes everywhere, especially because Beth had been baking, and she doubted if she'd get another chance at her book before supper. It was worth the try anyway.

Carelessly Melody clanged the forks and spoons into the sink and swished them through the water. Water and soap suds flew as she plunked in a kettle.

"Careful there, young lady," Beth cautioned. "I don't like if you get the window behind the sink all splashed up. If you do, you'll need to wash it after you're done with your other work."

"Forget the window," Melody scowled. She pulled the plug and wiped off the counters, then she rushed for the broom.

It didn't take long to sweep the floor. Melody skipped the corners, but she made sure that she got the middle and under the table. That was where it was most necessary anyway.

"Thank you, Melody," Mother said as she came into the kitchen. "If you'll empty the slop bucket yet, you can have time off till supper."

"Oh, Mother," Melody muttered.

Mother decided this had reached the limit, "That's enough, Melody. If you can't obey cheerfully, you may not read your book anymore tonight."

Melody took the slop bucket. It just didn't seem fair all this work that she had to do. By the time she got to the door she decided to just set the bucket inside the door and wait till after supper to empty it.

Melody sneaked back into the living room to get her book then she went to her room to read. For some reason she just didn't feel comfortable to sit in the living room to read.

Melody flopped across her bed and soon she was lost in the pages.

Crash! Thud.

"Well, whatever!"

"Who did that?"

"How ever did it happen?"

Melody leaped off her bed and ran to the kitchen. She couldn't believe the sight that met her eyes.

Father had come home and when he opened the door it hit the slop bucket and tipped it over, dumping the contents across the floor. It wasn't a pretty sight.

"Oh, Melody," Mother said. "Didn't you take the slop bucket out when I told you to?"

Her voice sounded funny almost as if she wanted to cry.

"It is pretty evident that she did not," Beth pointed out.

"I'm really, really sorry," Melody stammered. "I guess I was plenty careless. I never once thought of what would happen when Father came home."

"Melody," Father said. "You're looking at it the wrong way. The most important thing is to obey. Leaving it here instead of dumping it when Mother told you to, was disobedience whether I knocked it over or not."

"She got it dumped alright," Beth's eyes twinkled.

Melody glared at her.

"Okay, girls," Mother's voice sounded brisk once more. "Beth, you can finish setting the table and put the food on and I'll help Melody clean this up."

Melody felt guilty and a little worried as she helped Mother clean it up. Perhaps just cleaning the floor would be her only punishment. Melody thought that would be quite enough to help her remember.

Mother gave the floor one last swipe with her rag and stood up. "Melody, please take this out immediately and dump it."

Melody went. When she came back, Mother was waiting for her. "I want you to go bring your book, I think I'll keep it for a day to help you remember." Melody soberly got her book and handed it over. There was no chance that she would forget this in a long while.

11.

The Girls Learn Contentment

"Hello Mother, we're home," Joanna and Margaret clattered their lunch boxes on the counter top and shrugged off their coats.

"So I see," Mother set down the iron and reached for another shirt. "If I guessed right, you're hungry. There is some chocolate mix on the second shelf in the pantry. Pour yourself a glass of milk and tell me about your day."

"You couldn't guess," Joanna began, opening the cookie jar. "Sheryl had the nicest shoes I have ever seen. Please, could I get some like those too,

Mother? She said they didn't cost much, and her mother...."

"You should have seen the new dress Brenda has. Why it's simply gorgeous!" Margaret took up the tale.

"Well, girls!" Mother said as she carefully smoothed a sleeve. "I think we've heard enough. Maybe Brenda has a new dress and Sheryl has new shoes, but," she cleared her throat. "Girls, are we being discontent?"

"Let's see Joanna, you're shoes were new a month ago and they still appear quite serviceable, and as for Brenda's dress... Why I just made your blue one last week, Margaret. It fits nicely, doesn't it?"

"Um, yes," Margaret squirmed. "But you see Brenda's is lavender."

"I see," Mother murmured.

That evening before the girls were asleep Mother knocked on their bedroom door. "Are you still awake, girls?" she called quietly.

"Yes," came the muffled grunts.

Mother eased herself into the dark room and softly closed the door. Snapping on the light Mother looked at the huddled forms under the warm quilt.

"Joanna," she asked. "Could you get the book you were reading this evening?"

A frizzy head popped out from under the covers, "Which one?"

"Angels Over Waslala," Mother replied.

Joanna leaped out of bed and padded across the floor. She stopped in front of the ample bookshelves and scanned the titles for a moment. "Here it is," she said as she selected the desired book and brought it to Mother.

"Thank you, Joanna," Mother opened at the photo section. Slowly she paged through it while both girls crowded close.

"These people, Mother began, lived in a terror-filled region. Do you think they spent a lot of time thinking about the color of dress material?" She looked at Margaret.

"Well, hardly," Margaret admitted.

"As they endured the numerous robberies, do you think they were wishing for nice new shoes?"

This time Joanna squirmed. "Of course not."

Mother looked up. She could see she had made her point. "Tomorrow be glad for Sheryl and Brenda, but also think of the things in your own bedroom that many people don't have."

"We won't forget," both girls promised as they jumped back into bed and Mother tiptoed out.

"Was the book interesting?" whispered Margaret.

"Oh, yes," Joanna yawned.

"Well, Margaret fluffed up her pillow, I think I'll start reading it for myself tomorrow. This was a good lesson for us, don't you think?"

12.

Larry Learns Obedience

"I'm all ready, Mother," Larry hopped into the front seat of the car, his eyes shining.

"Are you?" Mother smiled at her eager young son and reached for her seatbelt.

Larry thought going shopping with Mother was a rare treat, for usually one of his three sisters went along. He settled back into his seat and watched the passing scenery.

"Oh," Mother exclaimed, stepping on the brake. "That looks like a worthwhile garage sale. Maybe I could find the bike you've been wanting."

Mother parked the car and Larry crawled out. As he followed Mother to the laden tables, spread out in a large garage, he could hardly believe his good fortune. On top of everything he could go to a garage sale and maybe find his longed for bike. His eyes scanned the tables.

"Mother," he cried. "Look here. Could I have this? I would use it in the barn." He picked up an eagle carved knife and opened the shiny blade with a click.

"Larry," Mother reproved, "You may look but not touch and your other knife is completely serviceable yet." She walked to another table and began inspecting the cooking utensils.

Larry stayed where he was. He tried to look and not touch, but then he saw something that made his eyes grow large. "What's that?" He wondered. "A wind-up car?" He looked behind him and saw that Mother had her back turned.

He picked up the car and turned it over. Sure enough. It could be wound up. He looked at the price tag. *Ten dollars*, he thought, *that's a lot of money*. Mother wouldn't give that much for only a toy car, even if it was ten inches long and brightly painted.

He looked again. Mother wasn't watching and the elderly man behind the cash box had gone inside the house. Surely he could just try it out.

Larry carefully wound it up and placed it on the macadam drive. Zoom! The little wheels spun

Larry watches in horror as his car
zooms for the road!

and the car took off, heading straight for the road. Larry gasped and lunged for the toy, but it slipped out of his grasp and flew out the short lane. Larry heard a screeching of tires and a CRUNCH!

Mother whirled around, "Larry!" she cried. "What have you done?" She looked at the road and then at her son. The pickup truck that had hit the toy car had continued on down the road and only the flattened remains of the car were left.

"I'm sorry, Mother," Larry faltered, "I just wanted to see if it would run."

Mother sadly looked at Larry, then she walked out and picked up the car. "Take this," she instructed, handing it to Larry. "And go tell the owner you will pay for it." She handed Larry a ten dollar bill and he sadly left.

The elderly man's eyes flew wide when Larry showed him the car, "What happened to this?" he sputtered.

Larry gulped and told him the whole story.

"Live and learn," the man grunted as he accepted the money.

Larry placed the shattered remains of the toy car onto the backseat of the car with Mother's other purchases and crawled into the front.

After they had gone a few miles, Mother turned to her son. "Larry," she said. "You didn't obey me and ruined someone else's property. For your punishment we will not think of getting a new bike for you for a while at least."

Larry nodded and kept his eyes on the road. He felt he had learned his lesson thoroughly.

Raindrops

See the raindrops falling
  Jumping up and down
Raindrops, are you dancing?
  Flaunting on the ground.

Little raindrops plipping
  On the wooden rail.
Feel the wetness flying
  Turning into hail.

Raindrops coming faster
  Dusting off the trees
Pounding down upon the roof
  Dripping off the eaves.

Raindrops sailing from the clouds
  Turning grass to green,
Land in perfect harmony
  Give a glossy sheen.

Raindrops end their hasty flight
  On the window pane,
Thank-you Lord; we say again,
  Thank-you Lord, for rain.

13.

Overcoming Exaggeration

Eight-year-old Laura banged the screen door behind herself and dashed into the kitchen. "Abigail," she called excitedly. "There are millions of ducks on the pond in the pasture. Come out quickly if you want to see them."

Abigail looked up doubtfully from her book, "Millions?"

"Just about," Laura insisted.

Abigail became interested and scrambled off her easy chair. She followed Laura out the door still thinking about her book.

"Hurry up," called Laura. "I can run much faster

than that. I can run about 30 miles an hour."

"You can not," Abigail contradicted. "There's no possible way."

They had reached the pond and Abigail could see at a glance that the 10-15 ducks on the pond were plenty far from millions, but she didn't say so.

"Girls," Mother announced, that evening after supper. "Laura can sweep the floor and Abigail will wash the dishes. After you're done you may go for a bike ride."

"Oh, great," Abigail started running hot water for the small pile of dishes.

Laura didn't sound so happy as she headed for the broom. "The floor is so dirty and cluttered, I don't think an ant could walk across," she declared.

"Why, Laura," Mother exclaimed, "It's not that bad at all. You'll probably be finished before Abigail."

"Huh," said Laura.

The night was cool as the girls started out the lane, but before long they were warm from their exertion.

"Whew," Laura said, puffing her way up the hill. "I will simply be dying of thirst long before we get home."

"I hope not," Abigail answered, "I'm sure it's not that bad, you're always exaggerating."

"You're too," Laura snapped. "I'm not 'always' exaggerating."

The girls biked the rest of the way in silence.

The girls enjoy their drink of iced tea.

They parked their bikes in the garage and opened the kitchen door.

"Ohhh," Laura exclaimed, for a minute forgetting their quarrel. "Iced tea!"

"Just what we need," Abigail added, drinking her second glass full.

Laura eyed the gallon pitcher. "I declare I could drink a whole pitcher full that size, right now."

"Laura," Mother reproved. "That's not honest. Say the truth and nothing but the truth. I've heard you exaggerating plenty the last while. It has gotten to be a habit, I'm afraid, and it must stop."

Laura nodded. "But Mother, can I sometimes make a guess? Like for the ducks this afternoon. I couldn't sit there and count all of them before they flew away."

"Laura," Mother said. "Think about it a little, a million?" Laura was silent.

"Try hard," Mother encouraged, "to be honest and break your habit once and for all."

"I will try my best," Laura answered soberly.

14.

It Pays To Be Careful

"Hurry, Ryan," big sister Crystal called. "It's time to leave for school. Whatever is taking you so long?"

"I'm brushing my teeth," Ryan muttered.

"You had all morning to brush your teeth," Crystal answered. "It's not fair that you are making the rest of us late yet, too."

"I had to find my science book. And it took me a long time," Ryan defended himself.

"It wouldn't have taken long if you would have put it away properly last night. You're so scatterbrained," Crystal accused.

"I'm not," Ryan felt peeved at his sister.

"Children, please try to speak kindly to each other," Mother said as she handed Ryan's lunch box and science book to him and opened the door. "Good- bye," she called.

Crystal waved in answer.

Mother closed the door and turned back to her work. It didn't please her with what she found when she entered Ryan's room. Dirty clothes were scattered on the floor or draped over the edge of his unmade bed. A pocketknife and a bird's nest were laying on the nightstand beside the alarm clock which was laying on it's side.

Mother sighed and cleaned up his room. *Something must be done about these untidy manners of our youngest son*, she thought.

When she returned downstairs she found Father seated at the table looking over some bills. He looked up quizzically. "Something the matter?" he asked.

Mother sat down across from him. "It's Ryan," she began, "he doesn't seem to have any idea of what neatness means, and I'm becoming concerned about his sloppy ways."

Father nodded. "I know what you mean. I've seen how he lets the tools drop when he finishes something, no matter where they might be lying."

Father and Mother talked for a while longer and between them they soon came up with a plan to help break Ryan of his careless habits.

As soon as Ryan came home from school and had his snack he went out to the shop. Father looked up from his work with a smile. "Did you have a good day at school, son?"

Ryan nodded.

"I've been wanting to talk to you," Father began, "about your problem of carelessness. It seems to be getting worse instead of any better. So Mother and I decided that we'll ask you for a nickel every time we find something that you did not put away when you were finished with it or when something is not done neatly."

Ryan didn't look overly pleased with this plan. Father went on, "and we also decided that you can ask us for a nickel every time you find something that Mother or I left lying around somewhere."

Ryan grinned in spite of himself.

"And now you'd better go feed the calves, Son, before you start your other chores." Father went back to his work and Ryan left the shop.

"I wonder how often I'll be able to catch Father or Mother?" he wondered, "I hope I won't need to part with even one nickel." He dumped the feed into the last calf trough and tossed the bucket to the ground, suddenly he stopped and retraced his steps. He picked up the bucket and walked back to the barn. *This might be harder than I figured,* he thought to himself.

But Ryan tried diligently in the next several weeks to become neater. And although he had to part with quite a few nickels, he also was able to receive several from Father and Mother.

Everyone was pleased with the change in Ryan. He was even pleased with himself as he had always thought he did not have the time to put everything away right when he was finished. He now found that it didn't cut into his playtime at all. In fact, he had more time than before because he did not have to spend time hunting for the things he needed.

15.

Heidi Learns to be Careful

"What shall I do next, Mother?" Heidi asked. She gave the table one last wipe with the dishcloth, then, from where she stood, she threw it across the room into the sink.

"Heidi," Mother reproved, looking at the water splashed window, "how many times have I told you not to throw your dishcloth, and for sure not when there is water in the sink. Now could you please wash that window before you sweep the floor?"

Heidi grumbled to herself as she washed the window. "I don't see why I can't throw the dishcloth, as long as there isn't any water in the sink. Why would I have to walk from the table, all the way across the room, just to put the dishcloth in the sink?"

She finished the window and reached for the broom, the dishcloth incident faded to the back of her mind as she planned her work. "I still need to weed the flower beds and sweep the living room and water my violet."

Nine-year-old Heidi loved flowers and the pink African violet she had received from a friend for her last birthday was her most cherished plant.

"I'll water the violet first," she decided. "Why, it has two new buds." She touched their surface wonderingly.

"Heidi," Mother called from the sewing room. "Are you still planning to do the flower beds this forenoon?"

"Yes, Mother," Heidi answered and headed for the door. She paused a moment outside and took deep breaths of the fresh spring air.

Heidi was almost done with the flower beds when Mother opened the door. "Heidi, dinner," she called.

"Alright," Heidi answered, "I'm almost finished." She gathered up the weeds she had pulled and threw them over the garden fence.

Everyone bowed their heads for a moment while Father said grace. Heidi hungrily eyed the mashed potatoes and fried chicken and took a generous helping.

"Thanks for the good dinner, Mother," Father

complimented as he pushed his chair from the table. "Do you have anything planned for the boys to do this afternoon?"

"No, I guess not, they can help you since the garden is weeded and the lawn mowed. They worked fast this forenoon." She smiled at Kenneth and Keith with appreciation. "Heidi can clear the table and do the dishes."

The door closed behind Father and the boys. Heidi stood up and began clearing the table.

"I'm going to lie down with baby Edith until she is sleeping. After you've done the dishes you can have free time till I get up." Mother washed the baby's hands and face and took her to the bedroom.

Heidi yawned as she ran hot water into the sink, added a squirt of soap and started to wash the small pile of dishes. It didn't take long and soon Heidi pulled the plug.

Heidi rung out her dishcloth and wiped the counter tops. Next she headed for the table on the other side of the kitchen. Absentmindedly she washed the tabletop and without thinking she threw her dishcloth across the room and into the sink. At least that is where it was supposed to land. This time instead of the sink, she had hit her prized birthday gift, the pink African violet.

Heidi gasped and quickly lifted the dishcloth off the plant, but the damage was done. One delicate pink bud and two large green leaves lay broken off inside the pot.

Heidi sadly looks at her ruined violet.

Heidi sadly picked up the flower and leaves. As she dropped them into the wastebasket, she decided, then and there, that there would be no more dishcloth throwing from now on. She had learned her lesson the hard way.

Snowflakes

Like a polka-dotted curtain
  Snow comes gliding down
Decking every branch and leaflet,
  Covering the ground.

White and pure, crystal diamonds
  Dazzling the eye,
Far into the horizon
  Meeting with the sky.

Snowdrifts made of fleecy whiteness
  Dotting every lane,
Snow with beauty clinging
  To the window pane.

Capping all the weathered fence posts
  Glinting with the sun,
Landing on the rooftops
  Snowy winter fun.

16.

Being an Example

Lisa paused in her potato peeling. "Those boys are so loud," she muttered to herself.

Mother was rocking baby Sarah in the bedroom and Lisa was alone in the kitchen. From the sounds coming from the garage one could tell that Lyndon and Karl were having fun.

"Sold!" came a tremendous yell.

Lisa dropped her half-peeled potato and opened the garage door. "Boys!" she scolded.

"Whatever are you trying to prove by being so loud? We'll soon have the neighbors knocking on our door, if you keep this up."

If Lisa wouldn't have been so upset she would have laughed at the sight. Five-year-old Lyndon was standing on top of the freezer and was doing his best to sound like an auctioneer. Eight-year-old Karl was on his bike and was collecting the bids from the invisible buyers. Neither of them turned down their volume.

"Boys! Did you hear what I said? You must be quieter!"

Now Karl grinned. "We're having an auction."

"I guess you are! Any one could hear that. Are you going to be quieter now?"

Karl and Lyndon nodded good-naturedly, but Lisa had barely shut the door when the auction resumed again with as much strength as ever.

"Little brothers," Lisa sighed.

"What is going on?" Mother came out of the bedroom.

"The boys are having an auction in the garage, but it's four times as loud as it would have to be."

Mother opened the door, "Karl and Lyndon, tone down your noise. It's not necessary to be yelling constantly."

The boys were instantly quieter and soon the auction quit entirely and they went outside to ride their bikes.

Lisa sighed. "They sure don't think it's necessary to obey me," she said to Mother.

"Lisa," Mother said gently. "Please, leave the

correction problems to Father and me. You can tell us if the boys don't behave, but to take the matter into your own hands will hardly help the situation. They'll eventually label you as a bossy big sister."

"They have already," Lisa mumbled.

"And don't forget," Mother continued, "you sometimes do the very same things you scold the boys for. As for all that noise they were making, I seem to remember a volley-ball game that you had earlier this week, and that had quite a bit of shouting too."

"Uh, yes," said Lisa.

"That is one of the things we need to work on around here, toning down the noise, but your good example is worth more then several scoldings. Try working on correcting yourself."

"But they can get so aggravating," Lisa sought to defend herself.

"It depends if you decide to let yourself get aggravated," Mother pointed out. "Try to ignore it when they gulp their water down or clump through the house with muddy boots and let me take care of it."

"I guess what you are trying to get through to me is minding my own business," Lisa decided.

"That's putting it in a nutshell," agreed Mother.

"I admit you hit the nail on the head. I have enough to do just keeping myself in line, without running after the boys." Lisa dropped the last peeled potato into the bowl and stood up.

"That's the spirit," Mother encouraged. "It'll probably be a challenge at first, but don't give up, and I believe you'll find both yourself and the boys happier.

17.

James and the Wash Line Post

"Look where I am," James called to his sister. Keturah finished pinning the towel she held to the wash line and turned to look.

"James," she exclaimed, "you had better come off."

James just grinned smugly from his perch on the wash line post. He didn't plan to come down, at least not just yet.

Keturah didn't say anything more, she just finished pinning the towels and washcloths to the line and picked up her empty laundry basket and disappeared into the house.

James sits on top of the wash line post.

James gazed about him with a satisfied air. The warm sun was shining and the birds were singing cheerfully. The morning air was fresh and cool and patches of sparkling dew still clung to the grass. Yes, indeed, this was an adventure. This was the first time he had climbed up the wash line posts. He hoped Keturah wouldn't tell Mother.

He didn't have long to wait for just then the door opened. "James," Mother's voice came clearly to him. "Stay off the wash line posts, you could fall down and hurt yourself.

James was sure this couldn't happen, but he didn't say so. He slowly slid down and then decided to go digging in the sand box with Rover. Soon he completely forgot about his morning mischief.

For several days James found other things to do in his spare time, but one day as he stood in front of the sink, rinsing the dinner dishes for Keturah, his gaze fell once again on those wash line posts. How tempting they looked and James loved to climb. He decided that Mom just didn't know how easy and safe it was. After all she had never done it.

And so he waited until he was sure Mother and Keturah were busy, then he slipped out of the door and sneaked around the house. Carefully he grasped the wooden post and hitched himself up.

Steadily he went, inch by inch. There. He was almost at the top. Then without warning, his hands lost their grip and he slid down the post, much faster than he had gone up!

With nothing to stop him, he hit the ground with a solid thump.

Stunned, he sat there, then he became aware of his hands. Many little slivers were embedded deeply in his skin and then James realized they hurt.

Sobbing, he got up and started for the house, but halfway there, he stopped suddenly. Oh no, he couldn't go into the house. Mother had told him to stay off and now he had disobeyed. He had never expected it to end this way. Well, James couldn't see anything else to do but go on.

Mother said when she saw his hands, "I'm very sorry, James, but maybe this will have to be your punishment for being disobedient."

And what a punishment it was! Every time Father pulled another tiny sliver out, James danced and wiggled about, while tears ran down his cheeks. But he never, ever climbed a wash line post again.

18.

Bennie Goes Camping

Bennie tossed another arm load of fire wood on the campfire and watched the cloud of sparks spiraling skyward.

"This sure is a pleasant evening," Grandpa commented, leaning back in his lawn chair.

"Yes," Bennie sat down beside his grandfather. "I've been looking forward to spending the night with you for weeks and I'm so glad it didn't rain." He eyed the small tent standing partly underneath the ancient giant oak tree in Grandpa's backyard.

"Bennie," Grandpa asked. "Do you know the sun is still shining?"

Seven-year-old Bennie started and looked at his grandpa in sheer astonishment. He glanced around him at the deepening twilight shadows. He certainly couldn't see anything that resembled a sun.

"On the other side of the earth, I mean." Grandpa poured himself another cup of coffee. "Look at the moon, Bennie."

Bennie tipped his head and gazed long and hard at the silent moon riding across the heavens.

"Do you see how bright it is this evening?" Grandpa quizzed.

Bennie nodded, "That's because it's full moon."

"Right," said Grandpa. "But do you know what gives the moon it's light?"

Bennie looked puzzled, so Grandpa said to him, "It's the sun, Bennie, the moon is reflecting the radiance of the sun."

Bennie was still staring at the moon. In fact, his neck was beginning to ache and his eyes were becoming blurred, but he was brimming with questions. "Grandpa, is the moon flat? I mean," he added hastily, "I know it's shaped like my softball, but are there hills and valleys on the face of the moon?"

Grandpa crossed his feet. "Certainly. If you look closely enough you'll see something that appears almost like a person's face. Those are mountains and craters that people call 'The Man on the Moon.'

"Oh," Bennie was beginning to understand.

"The moon has a relatively cold atmosphere so that nothing grows on the moon's desolate surface."

Bennie nodded, "Say, that's interesting, Grandpa." He leaned back and studied for a few minutes.

"And the most wonderful thing," Grandpa said feelingly as they got ready for bed, "the God who created the moon and us is still right here with me and you tonight."

Bennie rolled over in his sleeping bag. What had awakened him? Beside him, Grandpa stirred too. Although Grandpa was in his fifty's, sleeping in a tent with his oldest grandson was nothing new to him.

Bennie glanced at the wall of the tent where orange flames, dancing from the fire ring, cast an eerie glow.

A shadow passed between the tent and the fire, Bennie sucked in his breath sharply. The shadow continued around the tent and Bennie could hear an animal snuffling at the corners. Bennie sat stiff with terror. Could this be the cougar he had heard his uncles talking about? He had seen pictures of one and supposed if a cougar's features resembled a house cat, it would probably be about that size.

Through the cloud of his fear he could recall Grandpa saying, "The God who created the moon is right here tonight." Bennie relaxed slightly. But the

The raccoon is sneaking their marshmallows
in the middle of the night.

animal was still prowling around and Bennie thought he heard spoons and forks clattering. Had it hopped up on the picnic table, he wondered?

Bennie reached over and woke Grandpa, who opened his eyes briefly. "It's probably just a raccoon. Go back to sleep, Bennie. It won't hurt us."

Bennie flopped back into his comfortable nest. He told himself, *"God is here and He is taking care of us."*

Outside, the raccoon leaped off the picnic table and headed for the nearby woods with a fat, luscious marshmallow clamped in his jaws, but Bennie knew nothing of it for he was deep in a peaceful sleep.

19.

The Mushroom Hunt

"Hello," greeted Matthew and Alvin at the end of the Hershbergers' long lane. "Spring is just around the corner. What do you say? Shall we go mushroom hunting tonight?"

Steven thought fast. It was evident they were expecting an answer, but tonight? He had chores to do and Mom was getting anxious about the garden planting. "Well," he stalled for time, "what about Saturday? Then I'll have most of the day off, only chores to do, of course.

Matthew looked at his brother. "Will do."

Steven could not be quite sure whether they

appreciated the change of plans or not. Anyway they didn't have any business springing the suggestion on him like that.

But it most likely suited them just as well any other day. Their father had a bike shop and they didn't have chores like he did.

Throughout the week the boys made more plans and the trip started to look exciting.

"Let's take our bikes," Matthew proposed one morning. Steven didn't know what to think.

His bike most certainly wasn't new. Not compared to his friends'. Yet, Dad had said he just shouldn't let it bother him. Well he would think about that.

On Saturday morning the chores were done in record time as Steven raced with the clock. They had decided that he would ride over to Alvin and Matthew's place and go from there. That meant five minutes earlier then the planned seven o'clock start off.

"You're here," Alvin sounded relieved.

As if I wouldn't know that, Steven thought, slightly miffed.

The three boys walked to the bike shop where Alvin and Matthew stored their bikes. Steven entered the shop through a door which swung on well greased hinges. An impressive array of reflectors, chains, and bike carriers were lined on the wall awaiting a prospective buyer.

Steven wished, for the hundredth time, that his

father would own a business like this one, rather than a dairy farm. He was brought back to the present by the sound of his friends' wishful voices as they discussed something. Steven stepped closer so he could hear better.

"Why don't we take these three here," Alvin pointed to the gleaming brand-new bikes against the north wall. "We could use them and bring them back..."

Steven was about to protest, then he checked himself. These bikes were not his and if the boys decided to use them he would too. After all, it did look exciting to travel with never-been-used bikes.

Matthew made plans. "Lift them out the window and make a dash for the woods."

Squeak. The window protested shrilly. Steven glanced around in alarm.

"Don't worry," Matthew assured him, "and we would be the ones to catch the brunt of it, if it was ever found out."

Steven wasn't entirely convinced, but he helped hoist the bikes out and onto the grass below. Once he was outside, the cool breeze fanned his hot cheeks and he was looking forward to the adventure.

During the next couple hours the boys found a nice amount of mushrooms.

"Let's start back now," Steven suggested. "It's almost two o'clock and the chores need to be started a little earlier on Saturday evening."

The boys go biking down the road.

"Yes, I know," Matthew admitted, but in reality he was enjoying their trip and was reluctant to leave the woods. "We've never been back this trail," he said as they came to a fork in the road. "Let's explore it now," so saying he swung his bike to the left and the others followed. Matthew had the feeling they didn't really want to though.

About three quarters of an hour passed and the boys, who hadn't found a single mushroom since they left the main trail, were halfway back to the fork again. When they reached it they turned to the left and continued on their way.

The evening sun beat its rays on the boys and the squeaky sand made traveling difficult. After about an hour of this they admitted it; they were lost. Realizing it didn't help matters any and by now they had lost all sense of direction.

The sun settled in the western hills and dusk stealthily crept over the land. All was quiet, except for a faint hum that grew louder as time passed. The boys were much astonished to find themselves at the edge of a rather busy highway.

"Oh," Alvin exclaimed, "I know now where we are. It's at least a mile and a half to home."

A mile and a half? There was nothing else to do, so the boys kept on going. Long before they were home they had agreed that the next mushroom hunt would not be for quite awhile.

Of course, there was no possible way of getting the bikes back into their places without being detected. They got as far as the back yard when Father met them. As his gaze fell on the bikes the boys knew they had some explaining to do.

Steven got his own bike and peddled slowly out the lane toward home. No matter how much the others had in the matter, he knew he was at fault, too. Father would want to know all about it and then... Well, Steven had learned his lesson and he concluded that his friends had, too.

20.

An Answered Prayer

"What is there for snack?" Anthony asked, with typical growing boy eagerness. He set his lunch box on the counter.

"Did you have a good day at school?" Mother inquired as she brought cookies and milk to the table.

"Alright." Anthony reached for a cookie.

"Anthony," Mother said quietly, and a little sadly, "somehow Trixie got out of her pen this afternoon. She got in a tangle with that stray dog that's been hanging around here for a while. You know which one I mean? She is tore up pretty badly, I am afraid."

"Oh, no," Anthony groaned. "Where is she now?"

"I am not sure, but I did see her heading for the woods."

"I will see if I can find her right now," Anthony opened the door.

Mother's heart felt heavy as she watched her son walk across the yard. She knew how much his little beagle dog meant to him. They had often gone rabbit hunting or roaming the woods together. But now... Mother had seen Trixie and she was really doubtful that she would recover form her injuries. It looked bad.

An hour later Anthony came back into the house. "I found her lying under that maple tree by the fence row corner. I brought her water and food. Trixie drank the water, but she didn't touch the dog food. I could see she wanted to be left alone. She even growled at me when I tried to help her and she has never done that before," Anthony sighed.

"We'll see what Father says when he comes home. He will decide if we should call the vet or not," Mother advised.

Anthony took Father back to see Trixie after supper. "She is right here under the tree by the corner," Anthony motioned, but to his astonishment she was not there!

"Was she bleeding a lot?" Father questioned.

"No," Anthony shook his head, "But it seemed as if she was maybe hurt internally. I hope she hasn't crawled off to die."

Father and Anthony searched up and down the tree line, around the house and every place they imagined Trixie could have possibly gone, but it was no use. Trixie had simply vanished.

"We can get another dog sometime," Father tried to comfort Anthony.

But Anthony didn't feel like being comforted. He wanted his Trixie.

At school the next day, Anthony simply couldn't concentrate. Once he came home he searched the woods again and even walked through the fields looking and calling. But again his efforts weren't awarded and since it was getting late and he had other chores that needed to be done, he gave up the search.

Anthony was thinking about his dog again as he was preparing himself for bed that night. Was Trixie somewhere out in the cold dark night? He hoped she could defend herself from the coyotes if she needed to. Quietly he knelt. "Dear God," He prayed, "You know where my Trixie is tonight. Please keep her safe and heal her if it is Thy will and bring her back to me. Thank you, Lord. Amen."

With that Anthony crawled beneath the sheets and drifted off to sleep. During the night he dreamed he found Trixie curled up in the lawn chair on the back porch. She wagged her tail and seemed pleased to see him, and best of all she was perfectly well. Every detail was stamped vividly in his mind.

Early the next morning Mother knocked on Anthony's bedroom door. "Anthony it is time to get up."

Anthony rolled over in bed. That dream had seemed so real. Hurriedly he jerked on his clothes and clattered down the stairs. He went straight to the back door and opened it, and there she was! Just as it had been in his dream. The exact same chair, even though there were half a dozen other chairs on the porch as well.

"Oh, Trixie! You have actually come back," Anthony stroked her head and she whined eagerly. He checked for any cuts and bruises. But it appeared as if she was in perfect health.

"Why Anthony!" Mother sounded surprised. "It's Trixie, isn't it?"

"It sure is," Anthony beamed. "And look, she is a lot better. She doesn't even limp."

"It is truly a miracle," Mother agreed.

"I dreamed last night that she would be on this very lawn chair waiting for me and this morning I came out here and there she was! I prayed too, and I am sure that is why she was here this morning."

"Yes, I am sure that is why," Mother agreed.

21.

Making Friends

"Here's your lunch box, Rhonda," Mother handed the pretty blue lunch box to Rhonda and opened the door. "Enjoy your day. I'll be thinking of you."

Rhonda closed the door behind her and bravely started down the sidewalk. My first day at this new school, she thought. How will I ever manage it? She wished she had met the girls on Sunday, but they had moved on Monday and this was now Wednesday.

The school van eased to a stop and Rhonda opened the door. *Just where will I sit?* She wondered frantically.

"Hello," a girl from the front seat spoke up, "why don't you sit with me."

It was an invitation not a question. Rhonda seated herself beside the pretty-looking, blond, blue eyed girl.

"I'm Janet," She said, by way of introduction. "I'm in seventh grade, you are too, aren't you?"

Rhonda nodded, glad that Janet was so talkative. She began to relax, sure that if she had such a friend her day would go smoothly. It wasn't until she was entering the schoolhouse behind Janet that her nervousness came flooding back.

"You can place your lunch box here," Janet demonstrated, "I'll take you to our room."

Rhonda's eyes took in the classroom at a glance. It spoke of an orderly teacher with artful tastes.

The teacher, Irene, looked up from her desk with a welcoming smile. "Hello, Rhonda."

Rhonda managed a weak smile and wished fervently to overcome her shyness.

Janet took her over to the girls and introduced them one by one although Rhonda still remembered them faintly from earlier visits.

Janet pointed to a newly varnished desk. "This is yours, Rhonda. Shall I help you move in?"

The bell rang. Rhonda tried to carefully follow Janet's actions so she would not make a big blunder. *Oh, well. That didn't seem too bad.* Rhonda sat in her desk and watched to see what the others would do. When they got out their Bibles for

Janet shows Rhonda her desk.

morning devotions, Rhonda did, too.

And so the day passed. There were adjustments, to be sure, but she had a helpful group of friends who did everything they could to make her day pleasant.

Rhonda let the door slam behind her. "You were right, Mother, as always. I didn't have a terrible day in the least." And Rhonda told her mother how Janet had helped her throughout the day.

Mother listened patiently and when Rhonda ran out of breath, she quietly spoke. "Rhonda, you saw the Golden Rule today. By Janet's shining example you felt right at home, even if you only knew two or three of the students."

Rhonda nodded and skipped upstairs to change. She sat on the edge of the bed and once more recalled the events of the day.

Without meaning to her thoughts wandered back two years ago when a family had moved into their community. She had only been in fifth grade and the closest child her age was a girl a year younger.

With a pang of guilt Rhonda remembered how that day had gone. No one of Rhonda's tight circle of friends had done like Janet.

Oh I wish, I wish we had helped Abigail and been more friendly, Rhonda thought regretfully. *Now I know how absolutely terrified she must have felt.*

Abigail was the quietest girl Rhonda had ever met and it took more than a month to make her feel like one of them.

Rhonda's remorseful thoughts continued. *Why should I think of this now? Abigail is one of my closest friends.* Suddenly she sat up straighter. She had decided. *I'll write her a letter tonight and apologize to Abigail for making those first weeks so hard for her. It took Janet to teach me, ... 'as you would have them do unto you', even if I've known it since I've started to school."*

22.

To Finish Is Best

Andrea sat at the kitchen table. The morning sun, streaming in the window, slanted it's rays across the table and over her bent head. Carefully she maneuvered the tube of paint across the pillowcase, leaving an even line of pink paint behind.

"Andrea, could you please come here a minute," Mother called from the bedroom.

Andrea capped her paint tube and stood up. It didn't take long to run the errand for Mother and soon Andrea was back. She entered the kitchen just in time to see her four year old brother, Brian slide off the chair with a guilty look on his face. A few quick steps brought her to the table.

"Brian!" she cried. "That was very, very naughty." She picked up the pillowcase. "Mother just look what Brian did. He rubbed his finger over the wet paint and now it's awfully smudged."

Mother took a look. "I think we have some detergent in the washroom that would make it fainter, but I doubt it will come off completely. Brian, you should have left Andrea's pillowcase alone. Apologize, please," she prompted.

"I'm sorry," Brian said.

Andrea rolled up the pillowcase. "I don't feel like painting anymore." She stuffed the tubes of paint into a basket and took it to her bedroom closet. To make way for it she had to move aside a half-crocheted afghan and a dress that she had started to sew a month ago. She had become frustrated when it wouldn't go well and thus had crammed it into her closet.

Andrea re-entered the kitchen. "Are you still planning to go to town today?" she asked Mother.

"Yes, I'll need to. In fact, I'll be ready to leave soon," Mother answered. "It would be nice if you'd go along to help."

"Sure, I had figured on that," Andrea said, good-naturedly.

"Find Brian and take him out to the car with you. I'll be there in a minute."

"Brian, Brr-iian," Andrea called as she opened the car door.

"Here I am." Brian rounded the corner of the house.

Andrea helped him buckle his seat belt and was just getting settled herself when Mother came out of the house with her purse and keys.

"Okay, do we have everything?" Mother started the car.

"I guess," Andrea answered, "Where are you going to go first?"

"The grocery store," Mother guided the car onto the road.

They had only gone several miles when Andrea's sharp eyes caught sight of a small hand-made sign beside the road.

"Look, Mother, a yard sale. Would we have time to stop?"

Mother checked her watch, "I suppose so."

Andrea and Brian piled out of the car after Mother and walked behind her to the overflowing tables. Andrea walked along eying the different things, nothing really appealed to her until she came to the end of the last table. Her interest settled on a brightly colored box. "That's quite the mat-hooking kit," she whispered to herself, "I wonder if Mother would get it for me." She waited till she got Mother's attention, then she handed the box to her.

"What do you think?" Andrea questioned.

Mother inspected the mat-hooking kit. It looked like it had never been out of the box and Andrea hoped Mother would purchase it. Andrea loved working with such crafts.

Mother thought a bit then she shook her head and placed it back on the table. "No, I guess not." Noticing Andrea's look of disappointment, she added, "I'll tell you why once we are back in the car."

Andrea helped Mother place her bags of purchases into the trunk of the car, but she could hardly wait until they were back in the car and driving down the road. "Could you tell me why you didn't get that for me, Mother?" she asked.

"Yes," Mother replied, "I admit it would have made a nice project for you in your spare time and I know you enjoy doing things like that, but how do I know that you ever would have finished it?"

Andrea was astonished. "Oh Mother, I'm sure I would have. It would probably not even have taken that long."

"But what about that half-sewn dress you have or your pillowcase that has a half rose painted. When will that get finished? You must finish your projects before you start others or you might soon have a closet full ofthings you've lost interest in and they won't do any good in there."

Andrea was beginning to see what Mother meant. "I guess it wouldn't be wise to buy more such things," she admitted.

They drove in silence for awhile then Andrea spoke again, "Mother, do you know what I'll do as soon as we get home and I've put the groceries away?"

Mother glanced at her, "No. What?"

Andrea grinned as she said, "Finish painting that pillowcase."

"Good for you!" Mother praised.

23.

*Jeremy Learns
to Save*

"Mother," Jeremy burst into the kitchen. "Mr. Coker gave me five dollars for mowing his lawn this afternoon, may I keep it?"

Mother turned from the sink. "I guess you may," she decided. "You've worked hard to earn it."

"Oh thank you, Mother," Jeremy bounded up the stairs to his room. He opened his drawer and tucked the five dollars inside. He grinned to himself. Mother must be thinking that he was really growing up if she let him take care of his own money.

"Jeremy," Mother called up the stairs. "Father is

ready to go to town, you wanted to go along didn't you?"

"Oh, yes!" Jeremy leaped off his bed, and started for the stairs. Suddenly he stopped and retraced his steps. "I'll take that $5 along in case there is something I want."

"Where are you planning to go?" he asked Father as he jumped into the truck and shut the door.

Father turned the key, "To the Farm Supply Store. The part that I ordered last week for the tractor came in so I want to pick that up and get a few other things."

"I have $5 that I got for mowing Mr. Coker's lawn this last week and Mother said I could keep it. I brought it along."

"Why don't you just keep it instead of spending it right away," asked Father.

"Well, do you think I should?"

"It's your money, son. You'll have to learn to use it wisely," Father advised.

They had reached town by now and Father parked in front of the hardware store. Jeremy clambered out of the truck and followed Father inside. Father walked up to the counter.

"Good afternoon, sir. How can I help you?" the polite cashier asked.

As Father stated what he had come for, Jeremy's eyes roamed the laden shelves. He realized soon that his $5 wouldn't go very far, not with all the things he wanted.

Beside the cash register was a rack holding packs of gum and bags of candy. This was mainly what Jeremy was eyeing.

The clerk left to get the part that they needed. Father turned to walk down an aisle and Jeremy reluctantly followed. By now he had made up his mind. He didn't get to have candy often and hadn't Father and Mother said he could use his money as he liked?

Father picked up a hammer and a tape measure, "Look here, Jeremy," he said quietly. "These tape measures are only $4.50 a piece. Why don't you get one of these? It would be something you could use for a long while."

Jeremy hesitated a moment. He didn't really want to tell Father what he was really thinking of buying. "I guess I'll look around a bit yet."

Father didn't say a word, he just gathered up the rest of the things he needed and headed back to the cash register.

Jeremy paused before the candy rack again. Finally he picked up three packs of gum and one bag of candy. He placed it on the counter behind Father's things.

Father's eyebrows shot up and he opened his mouth as if to say something, then he closed it again. Jeremy squirmed a little, he knew what Father thought of his choice of purchase.

All the way home Jeremy chewed on his gum. In

fact, he chewed three pieces at once. That evening Jeremy actually went through a whole pack of gum. The next day didn't go any better. By the following evening Jeremy didn't have any gum or candy anymore and certainly not his five dollars.

Father sat down in the living room after supper, "Could I have a piece of your candy?" he asked.

Jeremy knew he was only teasing, but he would still need to say how matters stood. "I-I don't, I mean, it's all gone."

Father's recliner came down with a thump. "You mean you actually used all that gum and candy within two days!"

Jeremy nodded.

"Well, Son," said Father. "That wasn't a very moderate thing to do."

"I know," Jeremy sounded contrite. "I wish I still had my five dollars. I felt kind of sick anyway with all that candy."

Father grinned to himself. "It's no wonder. Take a lesson, son. Perhaps Mother and I had better keep your money for you until you learn to save it or otherwise spend it wisely."

Jeremy nodded again, "I'm learning already, Father."